The Magic Kerchief

by Kirby Larson

illustrated by Rosanne Litzinger

Holiday House / New York

Once upon a time, near a small village, lived a woman named Griselda. Each day she toiled alone in her field. Each night she rocked alone by her fire. There was one reason only for Griselda's solitary days and nights: she held her tongue for no one, not even the Lord Mayor.

"Paah," she would say as he passed by. "A donkey on two legs is still a donkey."

Yet when she saw her neighbors working in one another's fields and heard their laughter, she felt the weight of her loneliness. But her tongue had nettled too many for too long. Even the village priest left her out of his prayers.

"Paah," she would say as people crossed the lane to avoid her. "At least my words are not all vine and no fruit."

One night, as Griselda bent to her mending, she heard a knock. At the door stood an old woman wearing the loveliest kerchief Griselda had ever seen. It looked like a wreath of spring flowers on her head.

"Good evening," the woman said. "Have you room by your fire for a traveler?"

"My fire is meager," snapped Griselda.

"One ember easily warms old bones," said the woman, slipping inside.

"I suppose you've nowhere to sleep, as well," Griselda grumbled.

"Your words are again true. But don't bother yourself about that," said the visitor.

"Humph. And have half the village think I turned an old woman out into the night?" Griselda flurried around, making a small bed on the floor by the fire.

But the visitor was already sound asleep on Griselda's bed, with Griselda's quilt tight under her chin.

"It's warmer here anyway," Griselda said. Crawling into the makeshift bed, she was soon asleep herself.

Griselda's rooster woke the two women at sunrise.

"A thousand thank-yous for your kindness," the visitor said. "I have no way to repay you...except..." The woman untied her colorful kerchief and placed it in Griselda's hands.

For once, Griselda had no words, sharp or otherwise. She had never owned a garment so lovely.

"Just one thing more," said the woman. "There is magic in that kerchief."

"Then why not use it yourself," mocked Griselda, "and travel by enchanted coaches instead of tired feet?"

"There are many kinds of magic. I tell you: while you wear this kerchief, you will find great riches."

"Paah," said Griselda.

The other woman only smiled and was soon a small speck on the road.

As it was market day, Griselda gathered her basket and trade goods. "Riches!" she muttered. Had the old woman thought her a fool? Magic or not, the new kerchief was charming. Griselda tied it on snugly as she set off for the village. Her first stop was the baker's stall.

"Frau Griselda, what an enchanting kerchief," the baker's wife called bravely. The baker hid behind his oven.

"Paah," sputtered Griselda. She would tell the baker's wife that flattery could not freshen stale loaves.

She opened her mouth. But those words did not come.

"Your kind compliment is nearly as delicious as your bread. A loaf of your pumpernickel, please."

The baker blinked. His wife blinked. Griselda blinked.

She tried again. This time she proposed to scold the baker for last week's heavy loaf. "That last loaf was such a bargain— it lasted the week through! May I have two of your honey buns as well?"

The baker blinked. Griselda blinked. The baker's wife
quickly handed over the breads, then snatched up Griselda's
coins.

Fuming and fussing, Griselda clutched her basket close
and hurried away.

A young mother came around the corner. "Good day,
Frau Griselda," she said, edging toward the far side of the
lane. A pink and wrinkled infant fretted in her arms.

The babe looked like a sausage gone bad, and Griselda intended to say so.

"Ah, what a plump little sausage you have there." Griselda's hand flew to her mouth. What business did it have spitting out this babble?

The surprised mother looked again, as if to make certain it was really Griselda speaking. "Why, th-thank you. I do think he is rather precious."

Griselda shook her head. Precious, indeed! Furthermore, the infant looked colicky, a most disagreeable trait. Griselda's mouth opened, but again her tongue betrayed her.

"A bit of peppermint calms the colic," she said. Worse yet, her hands took on a life of their own and presented the mother with a bundle of peppermint—the very peppermint Griselda had planned to trade for more darning thread.

Griselda spun on her heels, holding her aching head. Who should cross her path at that moment but the Lord Mayor?

"Good day, Griselda!" He doffed his hat with a flourish. "How is your health?"

Before she could stop herself, Griselda answered, "My aches and pains vanish when I greet an old friend."

The Lord Mayor stumbled on a cobblestone. He rubbed his eyes. "It warms my heart that our friendship brings you such comfort," he answered.

Griselda clamped her lips as tight as a beggar's fist around a gold coin. She ached to tell him just what kind of comfort his friendship brought, but she dreaded what her traitorous tongue would do. She could bear no more. Griselda turned and fled home.

Safe inside her cottage, she untied her kerchief.

"Paah. Riches, indeed!" scoffed Griselda, tossing it aside. "The only reward I gathered this day was an aching head!"

The next morning, Griselda woke with the cock's crow. She carefully tied on her own worn kerchief and stepped outside.

"Frau Griselda," a voice called out. "Good day!" Up the path came the young mother from the village. "My babe slept the night through, thanks to your peppermint." She presented Griselda with a bouquet of wildflowers.

"But— It was nothing," answered Griselda.

"Perhaps to you," said the young mother, "but your good advice was sweeter to me than a whole cake of sugar!" She kissed Griselda's cheek and went on her way.

Griselda picked up her hoe and turned over weeds in her garden as she turned over the young mother's visit in her mind. At midday, she looked up from her work to see the baker and his wife huffing up the hill.

"Good friend Griselda, we thought you might enjoy some honey buns with your tea."

"But this is such a long way—"

"Not so long for one who loves my baking." The baker smiled. "Tomorrow I will set aside some strudel just for you."

"But, but—" Griselda's quick tongue was now thick and slow.

"We must get back to our ovens." The baker and his wife started off. "Until tomorrow," they called.

Griselda stared after them. It was all so bewildering. But the flowers did brighten up her cottage, and the honey buns smelled delicious.

At sunset, Griselda was surprised yet a third time.

Up to the front step swept the Lord Mayor.

"Dear Griselda," he called. "Let's sit by your fire and talk as we did when we were children at our nursie's knee."

Griselda could do nothing but invite him in—after all, they *had* been childhood friends.

Later, when the Lord Mayor had gone, Griselda could not help but smile. After years of lonely living, here she had three visits in one day! Perhaps the whole village was under a spell. Perhaps…She remembered the kerchief. The *magic* kerchief. She looked in the wash basket, under the hearth rug, and in every corner of her cottage.

It was nowhere to be found.

"Paah," she said. "No matter. Magic,
indeed." She blew out the candle and
climbed into bed.

From that time forth, though Griselda still toiled in her fields by day and rocked by her fire at night, she was rarely alone.

"Two heads are better than one," she told the baker's wife as they watched the Lord Mayor collect eggs. Griselda gave a broad wink. "Even if one is a cabbagehead."

For Ted and Kelly, who have worked
their own special magic in my life.
K. L.

To Kukla, Fran and Ollie.
R. L.

Text copyright © 2000 by Kirby Larson
Illustrations copyright © 2000 by Rosanne Litzinger
All Rights Reserved
Printed in the United States of America
FIRST EDITION

Library of Congress Cataloging-in-Publication Data
Larson, Kirby.
The magic kerchief / by Kirby Larson;
illustrated by Rosanne Litzinger.—1st ed.
p. cm.
Summary: Sharp-tongued and lonely Griselda gets
a magic kerchief from a mysterious stranger, and when she wears it
she can speak only kind words to the people she meets.
ISBN 0-8234-1473-6
[1. Fairy tales.] I. Litzinger, Rosanne, ill. II. Title.
PZ8.L3286Mag 2000   99-18846
[E]—dc21   CIP